GOOFY

WALT DISNEY'S

GOOFY
IN
GIANT TROUBLE

by

Don Christensen

Authorized Edition

WHITMAN PUBLISHING
DIVISION

Western Publishing Company, Inc.
Racine, Wisconsin

CONTENTS

Over the Tanga Straits

CHAPTER 1

A THOUSAND YEARS
OF CORAL

"Gawrsh, Mickey, do yuh mean I'm a sorta secret agent like you?"

Mickey Mouse smiled at Goofy's eagerness. He banked his small seaplane to a slightly different course over the Tanga Straits.

"Right, pal," he answered. "This

job is for the World-Police Orga-
nization."

Patiently Mickey explained the
problem. Here in the Tanga Straits
a ship had recently picked up a
strange radio message from a famous archaeologist:

". . . doing research at Tangarr
Ruins. Have seen the criminal
Black Pete and others near here.
Activities indicate some great
menace is being established. . . ."

Mickey sighed. "That's all that
came through. But when a man like

Mickey Explains the Problem

Professor Adam Tegg says there's trouble brewing, even the top brass at World-Police start worrying. You understand, Goofy, it's World-Pol's job to search out and zero in on international crime wherever it shows up."

"Yup! International," said Goofy, "whatever that is."

"They called me back to duty because I've tangled with Black Pete so often. By now I guess I'm supposed to know all his tricks."

With a frown Mickey added, "But Pete's always got some new

Discussing Black Pete

ones for me to figure out."

"Where do we find those ruins where the professor is?" Goofy asked, squinting hard at the nearest island, far below.

Mickey banked the small cabin plane again in a wide, landward sweep.

"Just keep your eyes peeled, pal —and hope we can spot them," he answered.

In the steeply tilted cabin of the banking plane, it was easy for Goofy to lean way over and look straight down.

Looking for the Ruins

"Goofy! Don't lean on the door latch!" Mickey cried, but it was too late.

Mickey's words were lost in Goofy's startled cry as the cabin door snapped open under his weight.

"Yeow-w-w-w—I'm fallin'!"

His long legs whipped out of sight, and downward he plunged.

"Mickee-e-e-e-e. . . ." he called out desperately, his call fading as he fell.

In an instant Mickey had flipped the plane into a fast wingover and

"Yeow-w-w-w!"

was plunging in pursuit of his plummeting friend.

Down, down, the plane roared. When its speed matched that of Goofy's fall, Mickey eased the ship over slowly . . . slowly. Goofy's flailing arms finally found a hold on the wing's leading edge, and Mickey pulled back on the controls. Like a screaming bird the plane came out of its dive—but not soon enough.

With Goofy's weight on the wing, Mickey realized he would never get the ship's nose pointed upward in

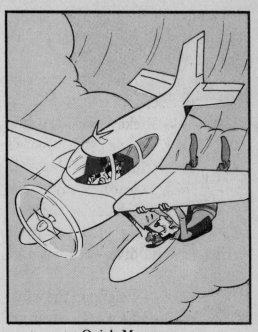

Quick Maneuver

time. Just as they were leveling
out, a high fringe of jungle suddenly appeared. Trees slashed at
the skimming plane, and its pontoon undercarriage was soon
ripped away. With Goofy clinging
to one wing, Mickey fought hard
to keep that wing tip high.

Now the white beach raced below them. When he realized that the
fight for altitude was lost, Mickey
quickly set the plane down in the
rolling surf. Goofy was hurled into
the sea, along with parts of the
crashed ship.

The Pontoons Break Away

Water soon closed over him.

Fighting his way free of the wreckage, Mickey called, "Goofy? Where are you?"

At the moment Goofy was sinking slowly to the coral-crested sands under the water. Mickey found him there, with his foot caught in a disk-shaped coral form.

Unable to free Goofy's foot from the entrapping chunk of coral, Mickey heaved the coral toward the shore. Goofy was pulled along with it.

Finally, when they were both

Stuck in the Coral

breathing air again, they stared at the coral shape.

"Gawrsh, Mickey," said Goofy. "Don't it sorta look like muh foot's caught in a little doorway?"

After a moment he wiggled his foot free and peered inside the hole.

"Yup, it's like a little thing to ride in, if it was bigger."

Mickey was busily chipping at the coral. Where it fell away, the dull smoothness of metal could be seen.

"Goofy!" he exclaimed. "It's—

"What Is It?"

it *was* a tiny spaceship—crusted with a thousand years of coral! Wow!"

"Aw, Mickey, nobody had spaceships a thousand years ago," Goofy objected. "I know that much!"

"*We* didn't have spaceships,. Goofy, but maybe this came from a planet where people were only as tall as your foot. Here—look at this!" Mickey held up two objects his searching hand had found within the little ship.

One was a tiny, spool-shaped device on which there were dial

"Look at This!"

markings. The other was a dome-like metal cap, the size of an egg cup.

Goofy's eyes brightened. He removed his hat. Then he placed the metal cap on the natural bump that was a permanent little extra on his otherwise round head.

"Look!" he said, chuckling. "It fits muh bump like a soldier helmet!"

Mickey wasn't listening. He was busy trying to twist the dial end of the tiny spool. "I wonder what this gizmo was supposed to do," he

Lightning Strikes the Cap

control into the surf.

"Mickeeee!" Goofy's voice boomed down from his new, incredible height. "I don't wanna be so big like this. What's happened to me, Mickey?"

"It's—it's that metal cap and the spool thing, Goofy! It's a control!" Mickey stared helplessly at his empty hands, then at the ebbing tide.

"Make me small again!" Goofy wailed. "Turn it! Unwind me!"

"I lost the thing," Mickey yelled. "But I'll find it."

"What Happened?"

Immediately he plunged beneath the surf and swam with his face only inches above the pebble-strewn bottom, peering desperately at every spool-like shape.

When he was forced to surface for air, he gasped, "I'll keep trying, Goofy—but there's a riptide. Maybe it swept the thing out farther."

"Mebbe a fish swallowed it," Goofy shouted. His giant hands came down and splashed beneath the waves. After a moment of frantic groping, he brought them up filled with fish.

Searching for the Control

But with fingers as big as tree trunks, poor Goofy could not even begin to probe for the spool control in the hundreds of fish he was holding. In despair, he threw down the fish and tried again.

This time his fingers closed on a shark and a small whale. He dangled them by their tails, trying to shake out the tiny spool—but apparently neither sea creature had it.

"Maybe there's another control device in the little spaceship," exclaimed Mickey hopefully.

"Maybe They Swallowed It."

Their hopes died, however, when they discovered that Goofy's great, stomping feet had crushed away all trace of the coral-encrusted relic of another era, or another world.

"Oh-h-h," Goofy groaned. "I'm stuck up here!"

"No, you'r̃ ꞌꞌot," said Mickey. "We just can't p꜀ꞈ When we find Professor Tegg, he'll ꞁꞈlp us. That control is such an important discovery that any country would dredge this sea to find it!"

"Gawrsh! One thing's fer sure," said Goofy, managing a smile. "Me

"I'm Stuck Up Here!"

being so big for a while—I can sure
handle that little ol' crook Black
Pete!"

"Hold it, pal," Mickey cautioned.
"You're too big a target."

Looking down from his fifty-foot
height, Goofy had to agree. When
his gaze lifted toward the sea beyond the island hills, he gulped
hard.

"Mickey! A ship's comin', and
I think it's somebody we know!" he
whispered.

Goofy peered through a slight
cleft in the hilltop ridge.

"A Ship's Comin'!"

The vessel moving toward them was a shabby motor trawler, riding low in the water. On its forward deck, a bulky, domineering figure loomed.

Eyes, fierce and searching, were turned in Goofy's direction. They seemed to bore right through the shield of hills. Goofy's frightened guess had been right.

The man was Black Pete!

Black Pete, the Pirate

Instructing the First Mate

CHAPTER 2

DANGEROUS CARGO

"What's the sighting, Cap'n?" growled Black Pete's first mate, Lugger Snipes, as he tried to match Pete's scowling stare toward the approaching island. Their course would take them close to the island's southern tip.

45

Pete snarled, "I saw dat mountain move—a bump in the middle moved!"

"I don't see it. Which bump?"

Pete stared again. "It's gone!" He turned away, scratching his head and mumbling, "Must've been just a landslide."

On the other side of the low mountain range, Goofy and Mickey were in a panic. Their first instinct was to hide. Goofy was trying his best, but how can a fellow hide when, except for the highest mountain, he is the biggest thing around?

Too Big to Hide

Mickey dived down once more into the water, and this time the search paid off. He recovered the control.

"Oh, I hope that turning it backward does something for you, pal," he said. "Here goes!"

He returned the dial to its former setting. Again lightning flashed, but this time in reverse. A jagged spear of energy leaped out of the metal cap on Goofy's head bump, crackled upward, and vanished in the clear blue sky.

A great quiver shook Goofy.

Lightning Flashes Again

"Mickey!" he shouted. "Look! I'm gettin' smaller!"

On his ship, Black Pete had good reason to stare again.

"Lugger," he said, gulping, "did ya see dat lightnin'? It went *back up into the clear sky!*"

As the trawler cleared the tip of the island, Pete and his nondescript crew lined the rail. They squinted into the bright sunlight of the southern sky, then toward the green shadows of the island. They were anxiously searching for an answer to the mystery of the

"Did Ya See Dat Lightnin'?"

backward lightning.

Goofy and Mickey huddled in sheltering foliage—hoping.

"Oh, don't let them see our plane wreckage," Mickey breathed.

Goofy could almost feel eyes squarely on him.

Beyond the reef, the trawler moved slowly past. Finally Black Pete left the rail. He looked again toward the clear sky.

"Well, at least it wasn't downward lightnin' hittin' *our cargo*." He paused at an open forward hatch. The hold below was filled

Hiding in the Foliage

with guns, munitions, and all kinds
of explosives.

Pete sneered, his evil eyes nar-
rowing. "I got great plans for all
these goodies. When we get this
load to the hideout, we'll have a
regular country store for crooks,
murderers and—heh—general, no-
good troublemakers."

"And you'll make 'em pay some
fancy prices, eh, Cap'n?" hissed
Sneer McCrag, the hawk-eyed
bos'n.

"Aye," Pete agreed. "And the
more trouble we peddle, the more

Enjoying Their Plans

customers we'll get. Dat's the way it is when everybody gets guns to use."

Lumbering toward the ship's bridge, Pete bellowed, "All right, lively now. Let's get this load away from this nutty lightnin' neighborhood."

As distance claimed the trawler, Mickey suddenly had an idea. "Goofy! Black Pete is our way to find the Tangarr Ruins and Professor Tegg. Look! Pete's course is toward the mainland. That means he must be returning to whatever

"We'll Follow Pete."

he's up to in the Tangarr area."

The question was *how* to follow Black Pete's pirate ship. They had nothing but the scraps of a wrecked plane in the surf.

"The pontoons!" Mickey cried. "We might be able to use them!" He ran toward the spot where trees had sheered away the plane's undercarriage just before their crash in the surf.

Their hearts soared with hope when they saw the pontoons. They were relatively undamaged. Within minutes a simple craft took

"We Can Use the Pontoons."

shape, and the two of them had no trouble portaging the craft to shore for launching. They had to travel fast to catch up with Black Pete.

Ready for Launching

On the Way

CHAPTER 3

FOLLOW THAT PARROT!

Once on the sea, battering waves threatened to tear the connecting braces of the pontoon undercarriage apart. For Goofy and Mickey, each riding one pontoon and paddling with wreckage from the plane, breathing became a series of short and painful gasps.

They fought to keep Black Pete's ship in sight.

Goofy gasped, "Why don't yuh make me a giant again, Mickey? Then—puff, puff—I could reach right out and—puff, puff—grab that smart-aleck ship so we could stop and get some rest."

"Hold on just a bit longer, pal," Mickey said, puffing also. "I think they'll be heading upriver when they reach the mainland. Then it won't be so hard to stay on their trail."

Goofy Is Exhausted

Their arms felt as heavy as lead, but they kept on paddling.

Finally Mickey gasped, "Look, Goofy! They must be coming to a river. The ship is heading inland."

Sure enough, when the boys' labored paddling efforts brought them to the turn-in point, they found a quiet tropical river spreading wide to meet the sea.

"Duh-h—at last some water that's not all wavy," Goofy said with a sigh, collapsing temporarily on his pontoon.

Mickey rested, too. "They'll be

A Quiet Tropical River

easy to follow now," he said.

After a moment they continued their pursuit up the quiet river. Just as they rounded the first bend, keeping close to shore, rough hands lashed out to grab them.

"Look out, Goofy!" Mickey cried. But it was too late to avoid the ambush. Pete's thugs were all over them.

The ship was hidden in a sheltered cove, and Black Pete was waiting on the deck.

When he recognized Mickey and Goofy, his surprise overshadowed

Ambush!

his triumph in their capture.

"Well, blow my bilge pumps," he roared. "I knew we had somebody tailin' us, but this is just too good!" Pete's sides shook with heavy laughter. "Haw—to think it would turn out to be you, Mouse, and yer knuckleheaded friend!"

"Heh—we just happened to be coming up this river," said Mickey, "because—er—well, our plane crashed and—"

"Belay that blather!" Pete exploded. This is the last time you *accidentally* butt in on me!"

"So You Were Tailin' Us!"

"Feed 'em to the crocodiles," Sneer and Lugger chorused.

But then, at the sound of a parrot squawking in the trees, all heads turned.

"It's our message-parrot, Cap'n!" Lugger hurried to the bow of the ship and permitted a gaudy-colored bird to flap down to a landing on his arm.

Pete hesitated. "Lock these two in the brig for now," he said finally, "and we'll dump 'em later—to the giant crocs upriver."

Even in the brig, Mickey and

The Message-Parrot Arrives

Goofy could hear the parrot's message.

"Awk! Old geezer named Tegg snoopin'—awk—around ruins near hideout. What orders? Awk!"

Then Goofy and Mickey heard Pete's voice, and his rough growl sent chills down their spines.

"Parrot, you tell Sam and the lads to knock off that old coot quick and permanent. Savvy?"

"Awk! Quick and permanent! Knock off the old coot!"

Goofy and Mickey shuddered.

They could hear the flapping of

Frightened Prisoners

distant wings. They knew that the parrot was on its way.

"Goofy! We've got to keep that message from getting upriver. Are you willing to risk the lightning again?" Mickey's face was deter-ined, but his eyes were tormented by uncertainty.

Goofy swallowed hard. He nod-ded. "I'm ready, Mickey," he said slowly.

He removed his hat. The metal cap was still in place on his head bump. Mickey carefully fingered the control.

"We Must Use the Lightning."

A slight twist—and an instant later a bolt of lightning stabbed through the heavy planks of the cabin ceiling, blasting a hole six feet wide

All of its violent force poured into the metal cap on Goofy's bump. He staggered and recovered. Then, with a quiver, he started growing taller. Up, up he grew through the hole in the ceiling.

"Give me a hoist up, Goofy, and let's get out of here," Mickey cried.

Above decks Pete's crewmen stared at the appearing giant.

"It's a Trick!"

were so confused that they did not lift a hand or gun to stop the giant. With Mickey on his shoulder, Goofy leaped to the riverbank and thundered off through the jungle.

"There's the parrot!" Mickey shouted, pointing at a distant speck in the sky. "There! After him, Goofy!"

"Shoot! Shoot!" Pete was shouting, and bullets began to zing dangerously close to Goofy's head and shoulders.

"We're not going to catch that parrot," Mickey shouted. "We're

"Follow the Parrot."

only fooling ourselves unless. . . .''

Mickey ripped two huge palm leaves from a tree as Goofy clomped past it. Next he grabbed some vines and quickly whipped them around his own wrists so that the broad leaves were lashed to him like wings.

"Now, pal, throw me as far as the parrot," Mickey said. "Hurry! I'll be all right—I hope."

Goofy did as Mickey ordered.

As he shot into the air, Mickey moaned, "Oh, this glider wing idea has just got to work!"

He spread his arms rigidly, and

"I Hope This Works."

the planing surface of the palm leaf
caught a soaring hold on the wind.
Ahead and below, the message-
parrot flapped along, unaware of
the fact that he was Mickey's
target.

"I'm going to fall short!" Mickey
gasped. "I've got to stretch my
glide."

Down he swooped and then up
again to gain extra altitude.

The message-parrot soon realized
what was about to happen, but he
could not escape Mickey and the
enveloping palm-leaf wings.

Stretching His Glide

Whichever way the parrot turned, Mickey swerved to remain above him and bear him down to a rough landing in the green treetops.

Hurrying through the jungle, Goofy called, "Mickey, where did yuh go?"

As he ran, a tangle of vines and branches clutched at him. Heavy limbs slapped him across his midsection, his eyes, and his Adam's apple.

"Here I am, Goofy," Mickey called. "I'm bringing down the parrot."

Hurrying Through the Jungle

By the time Goofy reached the tree that Mickey was descending, he was so tangled in jungle growth that he found crawling on hands and knees the fastest way to travel.

"Duh-h—the trees are thinner down here," he told Mickey.

When he saw the parrot, Goofy felt better. Mickey had the bird completely confined in entangling vines.

"We did it, huh, Mickey? Now those fellas won't get thuh message to—uh—hurt Professor Tegg!"

Mickey exclaimed, "But, Goofy,

"We Stopped Him!"

the same thing will happen to him if we don't stop Black Pete, too!"

Around them the dense jungle offered no likely trail. Goofy scowled thoughtfully. "How can we stop Black Pete if we don't know which way to go?" he asked his friend.

"*We* don't," said Mickey, "but this parrot still knows the way. Maybe he'll lead us to where he was going if we put him on a leash."

Mickey's thoughtful considerations were interrupted by the loud thump of Goofy's head against an

"Maybe He'll Lead Us to Pete."

overhanging tree limb.

"Ohhh," Goofy groaned, "I bump into everything when I'm this big." Mickey gave him a quick look of understanding.

"I guess it will be better if we get you back to your normal size, pal," he said. "Are you ready?"

Goofy nodded. He crouched, closed his eyes, and waited. He remembered his hat and removed it. Mickey slowly and carefully returned the dial end of the spool to its former setting.

Again lightning leaped up from

Goofy Waits for the Lightning

the metal cap on Goofy's head
bump to the clear blue sky. And
again Goofy quivered, then swiftly
returned to his normal size.

Neither Goofy nor Mickey noticed that, in nearby shadowed
undergrowth, eyes were watching.
While Mickey and Goofy turned to
the problem of attaching a vine
leash to one of the parrot's legs,
the owners of the eyes withdrew to
a whispered conference.

Black Pete was fuming as his
ship moved up the smooth, winding

"Keep Your Guns Ready."

squawking, "Gotta go! Home to Poppa!"

Mickey moved with the parrot, giving it free rein to choose its own direction.

"Come on, Goofy," he called. "This is going to be perfect."

Clinging tightly to the leash, Mickey floundered through the dense jungle growth after the flying parrot. When branches snagged the leash, he unhooked it as quickly as possible—hurried by the squawking bird's chatter.

"Awk! Cast off the anchor

Strong Arms Grab Goofy

underbrush before they spoke to
him. "Hail, Tanaga!" they said
finally, carefully setting Goofy on
the ground.

"Hail, Tanaga!"

The Leash Breaks

Goofy Freezes in His Tracks

abruptly that he jumped eight feet into the air. At the same moment, the tiger leaped forward.

Goofy came down astride the striped neck, facing backward. He hung on for all he was worth; he knew this was the only place that the tiger's slashing jaws could not reach.

To the natives, peering from their houses and other hiding places, it was an awesome sight. The leaping, thrashing Bengal whipped Goofy around like a rag doll. But somehow Goofy managed

A High Jump

to keep his legs locked around the huge neck, even though he felt as if every joint in his body were coming apart.

"Hallp! Mickeeee, where are yuh?" he yowled.

Then, out of the corner of one rattling eye, he saw a young boy in a tree. The boy was pointing toward the rough spot in the trail which the tiger had avoided.

"There is a pit—a hole!" the boy shouted. "Get him to the pit!"

Goofy misunderstood the boy, however. He thought the boy was

"Hallp!"

saying, "Get *into* the pit." Trying to do exactly that, Goofy sprang from the tiger. He landed far short of the hole and scrambled to his feet.

The tiger whirled in a blind fury, bounded after Goofy, and leaped. Goofy dived for the spot where he knew the pit must be. He fell short —flat on his face—and the tiger missed. Missed Goofy, that is, but not the pit.

With a terrible roar the tiger disappeared from sight, amid a woody splash of twigs, grass, and

Saved by the Pit

sticks of broken bamboo.

"He has done it!" a voice cried. "He lured the tiger into our pit-fall!"

Meanwhile, Mickey had back-tracked the trail the natives had left. When he arrived at the native village, he found the people gathered at the pit, praising Goofy. However, on hearing Mickey's story of the parrot's escape with its message of death for Professor Tegg, their joy changed to concern. They whispered together in groups.

Mickey Finds Goofy

"With your giant powers," a man suggested to Goofy hopefully, "you will conquer the evil ones?"

The boy who had called to Goofy from the tree spoke up. "Atoola and I will take you to the Tangarr Ruins—and swiftly."

He was a slender, dark-eyed youngster, no more than twelve years old. With a quick smile he ran behind a screening clump of bamboo. Several minutes later he returned, perched on top of a large elephant.

"This is my fine elephant,

Two New Friends

Atoola," he announced. "He cannot fly like a noisy parrot, but in the jungle nothing can stop him."

Many voices agreed. "Go with Hani and Atoola, friends. They will carry you to the ruins *and beyond —where the danger lies.*"

The way they said the words, however, disturbed both Goofy and Mickey.

Deciding What to Do

Atoola Marches On

CHAPTER 5

HELPFUL HANI
AND ATOOLA

Hani guided his elephant skill-
fully, clucking commands and
pressing bare heels into the tough
hide of Atoola's head. Behind him
sat Mickey and Goofy, with nothing
to do but dodge the low branches.

"Gawrsh!" Goofy exclaimed.

"Atoola mashes through everything practically—doesn't he?"

Above, a large plane was slanting down toward a spot not far away. Mickey scowled.

"There must be an airstrip up ahead," he murmured.

"Do yuh think thuh fellas in thuh plane saw us, Mickey?"

It was Hani who answered. "I am sure they could not see us, Tanaga."

Goofy protested, "I am *not* Tanaga. I'm Goofy."

Hani merely smiled sadly. "A

"Do Yuh Think They Saw Us?"

wise man would not dare to be a
giant in this age of guns and
cannons."

Suddenly Atoola crashed out of
the shrouding jungle into a clear-
ing. There would be no need for
Mickey and Goofy to search the
Tangarr Ruins. Where the green
web of vegetation had been cleared
away from ghostly walls of a past
era, there were unmistakable signs
of digging. A small shovel, a chisel,
and a pickax were abandoned near
a dying cookfire. There were indi-
cations of a struggle.

Professor Tegg's Camp

"This must be Professor Tegg's camp," Mickey declared. "Pete's men must have just been here."

Goofy swallowed hard. "Yuh mean we're too late?"

"Look!" said Hani. "There is the trail they left." He pointed toward a gap crushed in the surrounding underbrush. "Ahead there is a place where the river winds close to the volcano of Tangarr. I fear that is your goal, my friends."

At the place which Hani described, Black Pete's heavy-laden

"There Is the Trail."

trawler was being tied up at an improvised wharf that jutted out from some makeshift sheds. Behind the wharf a road curved upward between scattered trees toward a huge mountain that was topped by a jagged crater edge. Coming down the road was a man with a parrot perched on his shoulder. It was the message-parrot.

"Awk! Mission accomplished!" the parrot squawked.

Black Pete stamped down the gangplank from the trawler's deck to greet the man.

The Parrot Delivers a Message

"Good work, Sam," Pete said happily, but his eyes darted nervously toward nearby treetops. "Any sign of a big lug as tall as our mast—and that busybody, Mickey Mouse?" he asked.

When Sam's beady eyes nearly crossed in confusion, Pete explained how Mickey and Goofy had escaped in pursuit of the parrot.

"They must've caught him, and then the bird got away from them," Sam exclaimed. "He came flappin' in with a hunk of vine tied to one leg. But we got the message."

"They Must've Caught Him."

"Ya polished off the old geezer?"
Pete asked with an evil chuckle.

"Naw, but we got him locked in
the volcano," Sam explained. "We
got sidetracked when a plane came
in. That schnook, Zann, is up on the
airstrip now, ready to pay for all
the guns we can get aboard his
cargo plane."

"Hah!" Pete laughed. Then he
bellowed to the crew of the trawler,
"On the double, ya swabs! Get that
cargo up to the airstrip. We got our
first customer!"

Suddenly remembering, he

"We Got Our First Customer."

glared toward the treetops and added, "But keep your firepower ready for the mouse and that different-sizes goof!"

"Keep Your Firepower Ready."

The Secret Airstrip

CHAPTER 6

VOLCANO VENTURE

Atoola lowered Goofy to the ground beside Mickey. Through the trees they could glimpse the plane they had seen earlier. It was parked on the narrow airstrip cleared across a slightly elevated plateau that formed a step-down from the adjoining volcano to the river bottomland below.

From his perch on Atoola's head, Hani whispered down to them, "They are bringing guns from a tunnel in the mountain—and also up the road from the river."

"They're loading all that stuff into thuh airplane," Goofy declared.

Mickey signaled with one finger to his lips. "We may be walking into a trap, fellows," he whispered. "If we get split up, Goofy, remember, you will have to think for

"They're Loading Guns!"

yourself and make the best of things. Understand?"

Goofy nodded. "I gotcha, Mickey —think fer muhself."

In a whisper Mickey told Hani how he could help them in their search for Professor Tegg. The boy promised to do his best.

Screaming like a banshee, Hani prodded his elephant into an earth-shaking lope toward the river. The cargo-bearers on the road imme-diately stopped their hurried climb and stared toward the din that was suddenly exploding in the nearby

Mickey Whispers Instructions

jungle. The armed men on the airstrip looked about them in bewil-
derment.

With the attention of the villains
drawn to Hani's noisy flight,
Mickey and Goofy's quick scramble
across the mountain slope went un-
noticed. They soon reached a
shielded vantage point among the
rocks overlooking the airstrip.
Mickey told Goofy to keep his eye
on the trawler and the wharf.

Down below, Black Pete was
roaring, "C'mon back, ya trigger-
happy dimwits! It's just a scared

Scrambling for Cover

native kid on an elephant!"

He stalked toward a lean, hard-eyed man standing near the cargo plane.

"We'll have ya loaded before ya can say 'Jack Robber,' son," Pete said reassuringly.

The hard eyes flashed. "I am not your son, Black Pete. I am a buyer of your goods and about to become, with their help, the ruler of my country—Zann the First!"

As the loading of the plane was resumed, Zann glared at each case being hoisted carefully through the

Black Pete and Zann

wide cargo doors. His black beard jerked fretfully.

"I see no machine guns! I want many machine guns!" he snapped.

"Ya'll get 'em," said Pete. "And I'll even throw in an extra one if ya do me a little favor."

With a twisted grin, Pete continued. "We got an ol' busybody snooper locked up in the volcano. Now, all ya gotta do is take him along with you and dump him in the sea."

"Goofy! Did you hear that?" Mickey gasped. "In the volcano!

"Do Me a Little Favor."

We've got to get Professor Tegg out of there fast."

At that moment a man was leaving the tunnel entrance with an armload of rocket launchers. By darting behind rocks and scrubby mountain brush, Mickey and Goofy soon reached the tunnel and ducked quickly into its shadows.

They plunged uncertainly through the darkness for several minutes. At the end of the tunnel they came to a great cavernous room. It was stacked like a warehouse with cases of munitions,

The Tunnel Hideout

guns, and virtually every other form of weaponry. There was also a human figure to be seen.

"Who—who are you?" said an elderly man with strong, stubborn eyes and a crest of iron-gray hair. He was locked in a heavy cage that might once have been used to hold a captured tiger.

In hurried whispers Mickey identified himself and Goofy. Then he explained, "Your message got through, sir. We're from World-Pol. And don't worry, we've tangled with Black Pete before. We'll have

Finding Professor Tegg

you free in no time."

But the heavy bars and the massive lock on the cage defied their efforts. And shooting off the lock with one of the nearby guns was out of the question; all of Pete's gang would come running to check the noise. Mickey turned to Goofy.

"Pal," he said, "if there ever was a time for you to try that giant bit again—it's now."

Taking the spool control from his pocket, Mickey tried to reassure the puzzled archaeologist. "We'll explain about this lightning-sizer

"Try That Giant Bit Again."

later, sir. I'm going to make Goofy big enough to pull this cage apart."

Mickey pointed first to some crates and then to the high, open ceiling of the cavern.

"Goofy," he said, "when you get big, pile these cases over here to block the tunnel, then crack open the cage and lift the professor and me out through the crater topside."

"Awk! Awk!" The familiar squawk of the parrot struck their ears. Soon it came flying into the cavern room. Quickly it went out again.

The Parrot Overhears

"The enemy's aboard again! To your battle stations!" it screeched. "Awk! Man the guns!"

"Ready, Goofy?" Mickey asked.

"Yup," Goofy said, gulping, as he removed his hat.

Mickey stared. Then he gasped.

"It's gone! You've lost the metal cap!"

Goofy's head bump was indeed bare. He started to explain about all the bouncing around on the tiger.

"Scatter! Here they come!" Mickey yelled suddenly.

"The Metal Cap Is Gone!"

Mickey dived into the shadows of the storehouse area. Goofy followed suit in another direction. In another minute Black Pete and his men poured into the huge mountain room.

Within minutes they had discovered Mickey and, at knifepoint, forced him to submit to binding ropes. They came after Goofy, too. But somehow Goofy stumbled into a small tunnel, which led him to bright daylight again on the outside slope of the volcano.

"Gawrsh!" he sighed. "I didn't

Mickey Is Discovered

get a chance to tell Mickey I had put thuh metal cap in muh pocket fer safekeeping."

Sounds coming from the direction of the main tunnel entrance soon startled Goofy into action again. Leaping, stumbling, falling, and rolling, he descended the rocky slope. A split second after he reached covering underbrush, men were crossing the slope above. With guns ready, they searched every cleft and fissure.

Goofy edged slowly into heavier undergrowth. Finally he reached

Goofy Gets Away

the jungle and a point where he could see the main tunnel entrance. Black Pete was just coming out— with Mickey in tow.

"This is the one that counts," Black Pete said, laughing evilly. "He goes in the same bag with you, gramps," he added, speaking to Professor Tegg, who now appeared in the sunlight, a step behind him.

The professor and Mickey were herded at gunpoint toward the now almost fully loaded cargo plane. The crates of machine guns that were so important to the hard-eyed

Black Pete Laughs Evilly

would-be dictator, Zann, had been included in the load.

In his fern-draped hiding place, with searching men so near, Goofy felt terribly alone. Mickey's words echoed in his ears, *"If we get split up, pal—remember, you'll have to think for yourself and make the best of things!"*

Goofy tried hard, but somehow he could not coax a smart idea from his brain. The men were moving down the mountain slope now. One of them blasted several shots at something in the jungle. Goofy

Trying to Get an Idea

hoped he was not the target. He realized that it was almost too late for *any* idea, let alone a smart one.

At that moment the men on the slope began running toward a heavy, crackling jungle sound in the direction of the river. Seizing his opportunity, Goofy crawled away, frantically searching deeper brush.

"Good ol' Atoola," he gasped when it was safe to collapse for a few moments of tortured breathing. Suddenly he brightened.

"Gawrsh!" he said. "I think I've

An Opportune Time to Leave

got a smart idea. It's prob'ly what
Mickey would do."

Goofy could almost feel courage
surging through his tired limbs.

"Yessiree, it worked before. And
if Hani and Atoola don't get caught
by those mean fellas—I'll show
Mickey we can do it again!"

Goofy Gets an Idea

"C'mon Back, You Swabs."

CHAPTER 7

GOOFY'S PLAN

"C'mon back here, you swabs," Pete bellowed. "Quit chasin' that kid and his ham-hocked elephant!"

Zann's pilot, a dark-haired man with a face like hardened bread dough, easily hefted a large jute bag into the plane through the wide

cargo door. There were obviously
two squirming bodies inside the
bag.

Over his shoulder the pilot
shouted, "Have that goof aboard in
ten minutes or the sharks'll have
to settle for just these two."

After several minutes of frantic
searching, Goofy found Hani and
Atoola. They were even more confused and frightened than he had
been before he got his idea.

When Hani heard Goofy's idea,
his slender face did not brighten.

Live Cargo

"Yes," he agreed, "if Atoola and I climb aboard their small ship at the wharf, we may sink it. That is good. But for you to climb *aboard the plane* during the commotion, Tanaga, that may mean your death!"

Goofy was insistent. "Those two fellas won't know I'm hiding in thuh plane when they fly away. I'll let Mickey and thuh professor loose and we'll all clobber 'em. Then Mickey'll fly thuh plane to thuh police department."

A sound made Hani turn his

Goofy Seeks Hani's Help

head. "They are starting the great motors now!" he gasped.

He scrambled up Atoola's trunk, saying, "We will do as you say. I had forgotten that you are Tanaga-of-the-legends—a giant when the men of my village saw you."

"Oh, well, that's kinda complicated," Goofy mumbled, "when Mickey's not here. Yuh see, there's this little metal cap. . . ." He dug the cap from his pocket and placed it on his head bump.

The plane's engines roared louder. "Go," Hani urged. "And

Getting Ready for Action

may fortune be with you, friend—
if I never see you and Mickey
again."

As quietly as possible, Goofy
began to creep through the brush
that edged the airstrip. Soon Hani
and Atoola made their rush.

The lumbering elephant almost
reached the wharf before Black
Pete and his men realized what was
happening.

"Now what's that fool kid up
to?" Pete roared. "Stop that elephant! Stop the elephant before
he—"

"What's That Kid Up To?"

His words were cut short by the creaking agonies of the wharf. The structure was never meant to support so many tons of running elephant. Nor was the deck of the trawler.

"Kill that elephant! Shoot!" Sneer McCrag yelled.

"No-o-o!" Pete wailed. "He'll wreck the ship if ya just wound him—and, dead, we'd never get him off!" Glaring up at Hani, Pete ordered, "Get that big lump off my decks! Get him outta here!"

Hani pretended caution. "We

"Get Him Outta Here!"

must not panic him. If we are patient, perhaps he will get over this stubborn mood of his."

By this time every man, crook, and brigand was gathered on the wharf front or on the road between the river and the airstrip.

Thus, Goofy was able to slip aboard the cargo plane without discovery. He had just managed to slip out of sight behind some crates when voices sounded outside. The hard-eyed munitions buyer and his pilot soon climbed aboard the aircraft, moving with nervous haste.

Slipping Aboard

"Quickly, Gryzza," Zann hissed. "While they are occupied, get us airborne. Then all of these supplies will cost us nothing."

"Run out," the pilot gasped, "without payin' Black Pete?"

Zann allowed himself a slow, sneering smile. Then he said, chuckling, "We are merely teaching him that crime does not pay."

Leaping into the copilot seat, he snapped, "Hurry!"

"Hurry! Get Us Airborne!"

Surprise Takeoff

CHAPTER 8

OVERGROWN GOOFY

The turbojets screamed as the heavy plane gathered speed on the short-run airstrip. From the wharf and road there were angry cries. Shots reached after the runaway. Gryzza pulled the huge cargo craft aloft just in time to clear the fringe of jungle treetops.

Zann laughed. "We will pay Black Pete—by dumping that bag into the sea." Gryzza laughed, too.

For Goofy, reaching the bag quietly was no problem. His trouble started when he tried to untie the bindings around the neck of the bag. Somehow Goofy had never been very good at untying knots. And the fact that the door to the pilot compartment was open didn't help to ease his nervousness. He hunched down low.

It was Zann who turned and saw

Knot Trouble

fumbling fingers working on the stubborn knots.

"So!" he shouted, lunging into the cargo section. "Here is the missing link Black Pete could not catch!"

Goofy tried a weak smile. "I was just tryin' to get in thuh bag with muh friends—heh." Bending close to the bag, he whispered, "Mickey, make me a giant—quick!"

From the bag Mickey answered, "No, Goofy. We can't risk it up here."

Over his shoulder Zann called

Goofy Smiles Weakly

out to the pilot, "Gryzza! Open the cargo doors."

The doors slid aside and wind whistled through the wide opening to the sea, ten thousand feet below.

"You're going to lead the way, Skinny, to the bottom of the Tanga Straits," Zann shouted. "Get over there."

From his belt Zann drew a large revolver to add force to his order. But it would have taken a cannon to get Goofy even close to that open door. He leaped as far from the door as possible. Zann's shot missed

"Get Over There."

Goofy, but it sparked an outburst from the pilot compartment.

"No shooting!" Gryzza pleaded. "In this rough air you might hit *the stuff* and blow us all up!"

Zann pocketed the gun and lunged toward Goofy. With his overworked brain again thinking frantically, Goofy recalled his bout with the tiger. Suddenly he leaped above his attacker.

He hit the ceiling and came down unconscious, crumpled between several heavy cases. Zann reached awkwardly over the crates to get

Zann Lunges Toward Goofy

a solid grip on Goofy. It was difficult to do so.

"I'm coming. I'll give you a hand," Gryzza called out.

Swiftly he put the plane in the invisible hands of automatic flight controls. Then he leaped back into the cargo section, where he found Zann sliding a crate aside to get at the unconscious Goofy.

Together they dragged Goofy toward the open door.

"Wake up, Goofy! Don't let them throw you out!" Mickey called from inside the bag.

Dragging the Unconscious Goofy

About that time the foggy waves cleared from Goofy's battered brain.

He clamped onto the nearest crates as if he intended to become part of them.

"Make me a giant, Mickey!" he howled. "These fellas are too big fer me!"

Zann and Gryzza each had one of Goofy's legs now. Furiously they pulled him and the crates toward the waiting door.

Inside the bag Mickey realized he had no choice. He turned the dial

"Make Me a Giant, Mickey!"

end of the spool control.

From above the plane, lightning speared down. It spiked through the plane's broad back, and right through Goofy's hat.

Goofy quivered and started to grow. Soon Zann and Gryzza could not get out of the way of Goofy's enlarging legs, which were growing out the doorway. The would-be conqueror and his pilot held onto Goofy's pants legs for a few bewildered moments. Then, deciding the sea ten thousand feet below was the lesser danger, they let go.

"Let's Get Outta Here!"

Inside the plane Goofy was still growing. He had to scramble to pull his legs back inside. He pushed crates of explosives out the door to make more room for himself. The crates plummeted past Zann and Gryzza, who were now falling slower under the spread canopies of their parachutes. A storm of shattering explosions tore at the sea as the two men drifted down.

"Whew! It's crowded in here," said Goofy, when he was sure the growing had stopped. He had to remain on his hands and knees,

Explosives Plummet into the Sea

because if he stood up the hole in the ceiling would probably circle his waist.

The plane lurched sharply, as it had several times during Goofy's scrambles to get his legs inside.

"Goofy! Help us. We're sliding toward the door," Mickey called. Through the coarse mesh of the jute sacking, he could see the bright opening of the doorway. If the plane heeled over one foot farther, the bag would hurtle out. Goofy's weight, the lightning—or a combination of both—had thrown

"We're Sliding Toward the Door."

off, or knocked out, the automatic flight controls.

"Make me small again, Mickey!" Goofy pleaded. "Turn me back!"

"First close the door," Mickey shouted, "or fasten us to something. Tie us—hook us—anything!"

The shifting cargo was slowly pressing the bag out the door! Beside the door Goofy saw some strong straps with a hook attached to them. His huge fingers managed to jam the hook under the bindings at the neck of the bag.

"Make Me Small, Mickey!"

"Now, Mickey, now," he begged. "Make me smaller!"

But at that moment the plane heeled hard over in a sharp, landward bank. The bag plunged out the door, dragging the straps after it.

"No, Mickey—come back!" Goofy cried.

"Mickey—Come Back!"

"What's Goin' On in Dat Plane?"

CHAPTER 9

SOLO FLIGHT

Pete stared through his binoculars at the bag drifting down beneath a huge cargo chute.

"What's goin' on in dat crooked Zann's plane?" he sputtered. "Now he's even sendin' that bag of snoopers back to me!"

Pete glared at Hani. "And ya won't be able to help *anybody* this time, Shrimp! I'll take my chances with yer ten-ton pony."

Pete blew a speck of dust from the barrel of his pistol. Then he snarled to Hani, "Ya tell Big-nose to tiptoe off my boat quiet-like, or right now ya get to be the number one pigeon in my shootin' gallery."

Hani swallowed hard and gave Atoola a quiet order to step from the trawler to the wharf. With a quick glance in the direction of the descending parachute, Pete climbed

"Get Big-Nose off My Boat."

to the top of some crates stacked
nearby.

"Now—come over here and take
me aboard," he ordered. "We're
goin' after dat bag, and then we're
gonna *step on it*." He laughed wick-
edly. "Har, har! Aye! Dat's a very
popular sayin' where I come from
—*step on it*. And it's what this ten-
ton cow of yers is gonna do . . . or
ya don't live to tell about it."

Aboard the plane Goofy threw
his weight hard to one side. He was
relieved to feel the plane level out

"We're Goin' After Dat Bag."

again. It was sort of like balancing a canoe, he decided. Now, if he could only steer, he might have a chance, he hoped.

By hunching his face low, in line with the pilot compartment door, he could see forward through the windshield.

"Gawrsh! There's that pesky volcano," he exclaimed aloud. "I sure don't wanna bump into that!"

He stretched his great arms through the compartment door. His fingertips were almost as big as the semicircular control wheel.

"Gawrsh!"

Very carefully Goofy turned the
wheel until the volcano moved sideways out of his view.

Remembering how Mickey
pushed forward on his controls to
descend, Goofy tried that. But he
pushed too far and the plane slanted
into a steep dive! His fingertips
clawed at the wheel, trying to get
behind it and pull it backward to
bring up the nose.

Below, on the ground, Mickey
and Professor Tegg had survived
a rough landing. And in a twist of
good fortune, a knifelike shaft of

Goofy Tries the Controls

bamboo had slashed an opening in the bag.

As he wiggled out through the hole, Mickey's upturned gaze fell upon the diving plane.

"Oh, no!" he cried. "Pull up, Goofy!"

Like a frightened bird, the aircraft reversed its downward course and screamed into an upward swoop again.

The plane came up so sharply, in fact, that Goofy was thrown backward. His head slammed through the top of the fuselage,

"Pull Up, Goofy!"

and his hat was rammed down securely.

Blindly stretching one finger back into the pilot compartment, he found the control wheel and nudged it forward again. The nose of the plane came down.

"With muh head outside, at least I get a nice view," Goofy thought to himself.

But suddenly he saw something that made his heart leap into his throat. There were Mickey and Professor Tegg, climbing out of the tangle of the bag and the cargo

A Better View

chute, apparently unaware that Black Pete was advancing on them through the jungle, something metallic glistening in his hand.

Goofy's own hands stiffened with fear for his friends. A finger of the hand still in the pilot compartment accidentally pressed the throttle. The plane's engines conked out.

Frantically, Goofy ripped his way through the lightweight aluminum skin of the fuselage Wind knocked him full-length on the plane's broad back. He slid to the

A Frantic Exit

rear until his arms closed on the tail section. To keep from sliding off sideways, he gripped the tail flaps. Giving way to his multiplied strength and weight, the flaps swung upward—and the wind blowing against their upturned surfaces forced the tail of the plane down. As the ship leveled, this apparent control over the plane sparked an honest-to-goodness smart idea in Goofy's overworked brain.

He pulled the vertical, rudder section of the tail slightly to one

Terrifying Ride

side. In response to the change, the plane turned. Its powerless glide would soon be skimming treetops. Goofy pulled up hard on the flaps, hoping to extend the flight to the volcano.

Trying to Extend the Flight

"Look Out, Hani!"

CHAPTER 10

THE GREAT GOOFY

"He's going to crash the plane into the volcano!" Mickey shouted. Catching a glimpse of Atoola through the trees, Mickey cried, "Look out, Hani! Get away! Get away as far as you can!"

Black Pete leaped to his feet and

swayed back and forth on Atoola's back. He shook his fists at the nearing plane.

"Turn it! Turn it, you big lummox!" he bellowed. "Don't hit all those munitions!"

Hani prodded Atoola into a quick lunge ahead, and Pete went sprawling to the ground.

Mickey groaned, "Oh, no! No! Goofy will be killed!" He had leaped into a tree from which he could see the path of the plane more clearly. Professor Tegg scrambled up to a perch beside him, and together they

Atoola Lunges Forward

viewed the incredible sight of Goofy hanging below the tail of the huge plane, dragging his toes through the treetops! He looked like a child steering his sled with the pressures of his toes in the snow.

Then, tensing for the fall, Goofy let go. And during the brief seconds of Goofy's sprawling descent, Mickey acted. He twisted the control dial back to its normal setting —and lightning leaped away from Goofy.

When Goofy hit the treetops, he

Goofy Becomes Small Again

was much smaller. He bounced up just in time to see the plane explode against the side of the volcano, about twenty feet below the crater's edge.

Flaming wreckage showered in all directions. Some of the debris even landed in the open crater.

In the terrible minutes that followed, the Tangarr Volcano lived again. Flaming embers ignited wooden crates within the huge cavern room, and when their contents began exploding, the violence was beyond description.

Flaming Wreckage

The crater poured out flaring rockets for half an hour. By the time the earthshaking blasts subsided, government troops had arrived. They soon collected Black Pete and his terror-stricken renegades.

At last Goofy was able to talk. "Duh-h—I'm glad that's over," he said. Then added with a weary shake of his head, "Gawrsh! I sure don't like to be a big giant!"

Mickey smiled. "You're right, pal. No one should have to go through what you did—or anything

"I'm Glad That's Over!"

like it. I'm also glad it's over."

Studying the spool control, then the metal cap, which Goofy had removed from his head bump, Professor Tegg nodded in agreement.

Hani bobbed his head emphatically, too. "Too many problems when anybody gets bigger than Atoola," he declared.

"It is better that we never tell our troubled world about the secret of giants," said the professor quietly. "Everyone may not use it as well as Goofy."

So they placed the metal cap and

"We'll Keep These Secret."

the spool control between two flat rocks. At Hani's command, Atoola stepped on the top rock with one great elephant forefoot and pulverized the tiny objects.

As he departed, Hani smiled and said, "My people may forget our tales of the giant Tanaga. But now we shall have a new legend—*The Great Goofy!*"

Atoola Crushes the Objects

Other **BIG LITTLE BOOKS** Available
TM

WHITMAN *Big Book Adventures*

Based on famous TV shows

MONKEES

RAT PATROL

THE MAN FROM U.N.C.L.E.

BONANZA

GARRISON'S GORILLAS

LASSIE

STAR TREK

THE INVADERS

THE BIG VALLEY

VOYAGE TO THE BOTTOM OF THE SEA